SHEILA RAE, THE BRAVE

by Kevin Henkes
Puffin Books

PUFFIN BOOKS
Published by the Penguin Group
Viking Penguin, a division of Penguin Books USA Inc.,
375 Hudson Street, New York, New York 10014, U.S.A.
Penguin Books Ltd, 27 Wrights Lane, London W8 5TZ, England
Penguin Books Australia Ltd, Ringwood, Victoria, Australia
Penguin Books Canada Ltd, 10 Alcorn Avenue, Toronto, Ontario, Canada M4V 3B2
Penguin Books (N.Z.) Ltd, 182–190 Wairau Road, Auckland 10, New Zealand

Penguin Books Ltd, Registered Offices: Harmondsworth, Middlesex, England

First published in the United States of America by Greenwillow Books, 1987
First published in Picture Puffins, 1988 by
arrangement with William Morrow and Company, Inc.
7 9 10 8 6
Copyright © Kevin Henkes, 1987
All rights reserved
Library of Congress Catalog Card No: 87-62370

For Gretchen

Sheila Rae wasn't afraid of anything.

She wasn't afraid of the dark.

She wasn't afraid of thunder and lightning.

And she wasn't afraid of the big black dog
at the end of the block.

At dinner, Sheila Rae made believe that the cherries
in her fruit cocktail were the eyes of dead bears,
and she ate five of them.

At school, Sheila Rae giggled when the principal walked by.

And when her classmate Wendell stole her jump rope during recess, Sheila Rae tied him up until the bell rang. "I am very brave," Sheila Rae said, patting herself on the back.

Sheila Rae stepped on every crack in the sidewalk without fear.

When her sister, Louise, said there was a monster in the closet, Sheila Rae attacked it.

And she rode her bicycle no-handed with her eyes closed.
"Yea! Yea! Sheila Rae!" her friends yelled,
clapping their hands.

One day, Sheila Rae decided to walk home from school a new way. Louise was afraid to. "You're too brave for me," Louise said.

"You're always such a scaredy-cat," Sheila Rae called.
"Am not," whispered Louise.

Sheila Rae started off, skipping.
"I am brave," she sang. "I am fearless."

She stepped on every crack.

She walked backwards with her eyes closed.

She growled at stray dogs,

and bared her teeth at stray cats.

And she pretended that the trees were evil creatures.
She climbed up them and broke their fingers off.
Snap, snap, snap.

Sheila Rae walked and walked.

She turned corners.

She crossed streets.

It suddenly occurred to Sheila Rae
that nothing looked familiar.

Sheila Rae heard frightening noises.
They sounded worse than thunder.

She thought horrible thoughts.
They were worse than anything she had ever imagined.
"I am brave," Sheila Rae tried to convince herself.
"I am fearless."

The sounds became more frightening.
The thoughts became more horrible.
Sheila Rae sat down on a rock and cried.
"Help," she sniffed.

She thought of her mother and her father and Louise.
"Mother! Father! Louise!" she cried.

"Here I am," a voice said.

"Louise!" Sheila Rae hugged her sister.
"We're lost," Sheila Rae said.
"No, we're not," said Louise. "I know the
way home. Follow me!"

Louise stepped on every crack.

She walked backwards with her eyes closed.

She growled at stray dogs, and bared
her teeth at stray cats.

And she pretended that the trees were evil creatures.
She jumped up and broke their fingers off.
Snap, snap, snap.
Sheila Rae walked quietly behind her.

They walked and walked.

They crossed streets.

They turned corners.

Soon their house could be seen between the trees.
Sheila Rae grabbed Louise and dashed up the street.

When they reached their own yard and the gate
was closed behind them, Sheila Rae said,
"Louise, you are brave. You are fearless."

"We both are," said Louise.
  And they walked backwards into the house
  with their eyes closed.